Battle of
the Bunks

STORM CLIFF
STABLES

PEABODY INSTITUTE
LIBRARY
DANVERS, MASS.

by Lisa Mullarkey
Illustrated by Paula Franco

Calico

An Imprint of Magic Wagon
abdopublishing.com

To Ainsley Geddis: You're the Boss of Applesauce! —LM

This book is dedicated to my very first friend, Pom. —PF

abdopublishing.com

Published by Magic Wagon, a division of ABDO, PO Box 398166, Minneapolis, Minnesota 55439. Copyright © 2017 by Abdo Consulting Group, Inc. International copyrights reserved in all countries. No part of this book may be reproduced in any form without written permission from the publisher. Calico™ is a trademark and logo of Magic Wagon.

Printed in the United States of America, North Mankato, Minnesota.
052016
092016

 **THIS BOOK CONTAINS RECYCLED MATERIALS**

Written by Lisa Mullarkey
Illustrated by Paula Franco
Edited by Tamara L. Britton, Megan M. Gunderson & Bridget O'Brien
Designed by Christina Doffing
Art Directed by Candice Keimig

Library of Congress Cataloging-in-Publication Data

Names: Mullarkey, Lisa, author. | Franco, Paula, illustrator. | Mullarkey, Lisa. Storm Cliff Stables.
Title: Battle of the bunks / by Lisa Mullarkey ; illustrated by Paula Franco.
Description: Minneapolis, MN : Magic Wagon, [2017] | Series: Storm Cliff Stables | Summary: At Storm Cliff Stables, Ainsley and her cabin-mates, the Four Horseketeers, are engaged in a pranking battle with another cabin group called the Core Four, but they soon find that this kind of activity can get out of hand--especially when somebody outside the group starts pranking everybody.
Identifiers: LCCN 2016003363 (print) | LCCN 2016004793 (ebook) | ISBN 9781624021626 (lib. bdg.) | ISBN 9781680790412 (ebook)
Subjects: LCSH: Riding schools--Juvenile fiction. | Practical jokes--Juvenile fiction. | Horses--Juvenile fiction. | Friendship--Juvenile fiction. | CYAC: Mystery and detective stories. | Practical jokes--Fiction. | Horses--Fiction. | Friendship--Fiction. | Camps--Fiction. | GSAFD: Mystery fiction.
Classification: LCC PZ7.M91148 Bat 2016 (print) | LCC PZ7.M91148 (ebook) | DDC 813.6--dc23
LC record available at http://lccn.loc.gov/2016003363

Table of Contents

I stood on my tiptoes and peeked in the window. "The coast is clear except for a couple of cobwebs."

I lifted the screen off its tracks and leaned it against the cabin.

Ryleigh's, Cassidy's, and Khadija's eyes darted from me, to the window, then back to me.

I bent down and cupped my hands. "Climb on, someone. Let the pranks begin!"

"I'll go first, Ainsley," said Ryleigh.

She jammed her foot into my palm and launched her body up into the window. She teetered for a few seconds before jumping down.

"Mission accomplished," I said. "One in. Three to go."

Khadija tugged nervously on her hijab. "Aunt Jane better not find out."

"She won't find out," I said. "Trust me."

Aunt Jane owns Storm Cliff Stables. Even though she isn't our real aunt, she considers every camper part of her family.

Khadija shoved her hands into her pockets. "I hope you're right."

I pushed my glasses up. "We're not the first ones to pull a prank at camp, you know." I bent down again. "Don't be such a baby."

Khadija hesitated.

"Use my hands as a springboard like Ryleigh did," I said. "Step on and lift up in one quick motion."

In seconds, Khadija was inside too.

There was a *crack-crack-crack* in the woods behind us. Cassidy and I scanned the area.

A second later, a deer popped its head through some bushes and dashed toward the clearing.

Cassidy looked relieved until Carly, a younger camper, popped her head up too.

"Whatcha doing?" she asked.

"Buzz off," I said.

Carly twirled her hair around her finger. "I'm really good at pranking people, ya know. Let me help."

"No way," I mumbled. "We don't want a nine-year-old baby helping us."

She puffed out her bottom lip. "I'm not a baby. I'm nine and a *half*."

"Trust me," I said. "You're still a B-A-B-Y." I shook my finger in front of her face. "Don't go blabbing to anyone that you saw us here. Got it?"

She stuck her tongue out and marched away. "Got it."

Cassidy winced. "Are you sure you've pulled pranks like this before?"

I shrugged. "Not exactly . . ."

Her shoulders drooped. "You said everyone

pulls camp pranks! I don't want to get in trouble."

I crouched down and held out my hands. "You won't. Promise."

But Cassidy was so tall that she didn't need my help. She gripped the windowsill and pulled herself through the window.

Then the three of them grabbed my arms and pulled me inside.

I tapped the poster of Anna Wainwright on the wall. She's an Olympic gold medalist. "When did Avery get this autographed?" I turned to Cassidy. "Avery might try out for the US Equestrian Team."

"She's that good?" asked Cassidy.

I shrugged. "Yeah. But I'm better. Way better."

Khadija gasped. "Ainsley!"

"I'm just telling it like it is," I said. "Nothing wrong with that."

Ryleigh studied the room. "Do we have to turn everything upside down?"

"Everything," I said.

Khadija frowned. "What about the bunks?"

I tried to lift the metal frame. "They're too heavy to turn over, but we can flip the mattresses. Keep the sheets and blankets on and tuck the pillow under the mattress."

Ryleigh giggled. "They'll sure sleep tight in these beds!"

"We better hurry," I said. "If we're late for our lessons, Aunt Jane and Layla will be out looking for us."

Layla is our cabin's counselor.

Cassidy walked over to the poster to get a closer look.

"Be careful with that," I warned. "Don't rip it. Avery will throw a fit!"

Cassidy peeled each corner away from the wall and then rehung it upside down.

"Perfect," I said. "Let's clear off the desk. Toss everything onto the bunk for now."

After it was emptied, we flipped the desk over so the legs faced the ceiling. Then we put everything back on the bottom side of it.

I grabbed a blue mug that had a picture of Avery and Sapphire on it. It was stuffed with gel pens and colored pencils. "Up and over," I said. The pens and pencils spilled out and some of them rolled under the bunk.

Ryleigh took care of the picture frames. Before she turned each one over, she waved at the people and the horses in the photos. "Say cheese!" She giggled. "Or neigh!"

Khadija gathered the books and magazines. "*Black Beauty. Misty of Chincoteague. Horse & Rider.*" She faced the covers down on the desk and then grabbed the drawing books.

"These must be Jaelyn's," Khadija said.

"Just make sure nothing gets ruined," I reminded her.

I glanced around the room and spied Esha's nail polish. I stood each one up on its lid. "They look like a capsized multicolored rainbow."

Khadija fiddled with the lamp. She unscrewed the bulb and took off the shade. Once she turned the lamp over, she put the shade on its base.

Then we attacked the bulletin board. As soon as we spun it around, papers and pictures fluttered to the floor. We picked them up and tacked each one upside down.

Ryleigh held up Bree's black satchel and hesitated. "What should I do with this? Dr. Samuels gave it to Bree."

I peeked inside. "I'm not sure what's inside, but it gets the flip-flop treatment too."

Khadija and Cassidy took care of the bathroom. They turned the smiley face shower curtain upside down and overturned the soaps and lotions and placed them in a line, smallest to largest.

To finish off the bathroom, I reached into the shower and pushed the nozzle up so it faced the ceiling. "Ta-da! The cherry on top of the sundae!"

Then we looked under the beds. There were suitcases and plastic bins with socks and sweatshirts stuffed inside. We slid everything out and turned them over, too.

"Don't forget to flip any dust bunnies you find," I said.

Ryleigh smiled as she scooched farther under the bed. "I see Jaelyn's art case." She pulled it out and held it up.

"Don't just hold it up," I said. "Flip it."

Ryleigh slid it back under the wrong way.

After another twenty minutes, we were done.

"We forgot one thing," I said. I grabbed the chair and put it next to the door. I stood on it and reached for the horseshoe hanging above the door frame.

"I wouldn't do that if I were you," warned Khadija. "It'll bring them bad luck."

"I don't believe in that stuff," I said.

"Or it could bring you bad luck," said Ryleigh. "Are you sure you want to do that, Ainsley?"

I hesitated for a few seconds before turning it around. "Bad luck, shmad luck. I don't believe in bad luck at all."

Just then, a boom of thunder erupted! We looked toward the window and saw a black cat sitting on the ledge of the windowsill.

A chill ran up my spine. "I . . . I don't believe in bad luck at all," I repeated.

Suddenly, the poster of Anna Wainwright peeled off the wall and fell to the ground.

I took a deep breath and crossed my fingers.

Okay . . . maybe I believed in a little bad luck after all.

I shooed the cat away. "Let's get out of here." I opened the door and looked up. "It's raining cats and dogs! Run between the raindrops!"

We bolted to the stables. By the time we got there, we were soaked.

"No lessons today," said Layla. She pointed to the stalls. "But I know of some horses that would love grooming time."

Khadija's face lit up. "Silver Moon deserves some TLC." She grabbed Twinkle Toes Hoof Glitter. "I'm going to fancy her up."

Ryleigh turned to Cassidy. "I'm mucking out Butterscotch's stall. Wanna help?"

Butterscotch is a palomino quarter horse stallion. His mane and tail are the most beautiful flaxen color I've ever seen.

"If I help you with Butterscotch's stall now, will you help me with Maverick's sometime this week?" asked Cassidy.

Cassidy loves Maverick. Although no one is allowed to ride him, she spends an hour grooming and singing to him every day. Some of the campers are calling him "Cassidy's horse."

Ryleigh shook Cassidy's hand. "Deal."

My eyes lit up when I saw my horse. She's a black Percheron mare and over eighteen hands tall . . . the biggest horse at Storm Cliff Stables. "I missed you, Minka." I hugged her neck.

Layla stopped by with a new grooming brush. She patted Minka on the nose and gave her a piece of apple. Minka thanked Layla by brushing her nose against her cheek.

"She likes you," I said.

Then Minka pressed harder against Layla's cheek.

Layla gave her another chunk. "That's her way of telling me she wants another piece of apple. She's bossy, Ainsley. Just like you."

According to Aunt Jane, Minka is a handful. And according to my mom, so am I. So we're perfect together!

I put my arms around her neck and squeezed her gently. "We just pulled a funny prank, Minka."

Carly popped her head over the side of the wall. "It wasn't that funny."

I swung my head around. "Carly Jacobs! Mind your business. No blabbing! Got it?"

"If I don't tattle, will you let me pull a prank with you?" She rubbed her hands together. "I love pranks!"

"N-O spells no," I said.

She reached inside her pocket, pulled out a worm, and dangled it in the air. "Doesn't this little guy remind you of Gertie?"

Gertie was her pet snake at camp last year.

"Avery hates worms. Wouldn't it be funny if I put this in her bed?" Carly asked.

"That would be mean," I said.

She dropped it into her palm and watched it wiggle. "If you change your mind, let me know. Okay?" She skipped out of the stall.

I patted Minka's belly and then gave it a good scratching. "Can I tell you a secret, Minka? We ripped Avery's poster. But it was an accident." I scratched her belly again. "You believe me, don't ya?"

Minka whinnied.

For agreeing, I gave her a peppermint candy and braided her tail.

But not everyone believed me.

Avery, Bree, Jaelyn, and Esha came stomping into the stable.

"You ruined my poster," said Avery.

"And my paints!" said Jaelyn.

Khadija, Cassidy, and Ryleigh rushed over as soon as they saw the Core Four.

"What are you talking about?" I said. "And why are you back so early?"

Esha pointed to her soggy clothes. "It's rainin'. We've been back long enough to see the prank you pulled."

I tilted my head and rubbed my chin like I was confused. "What prank?"

"The one where you flipped my art box and made my paints spill all over the inside of the box and onto the floor," said Jaelyn. "The lids weren't on them."

"Oh no!" said Ryleigh. "Sorry!"

Cassidy tried to cover Ryleigh's mouth but it was too late.

Ryleigh froze. "Oops. Did I just say that?"

Khadija did a facepalm.

Avery put her hands on her hips. "So you admit it?"

"Well, Miss Bigmouth just told you," I said. "So, yeah. But . . ."

"But what?" asked Esha.

"But it was supposed to be a funny prank. We thought everyone would laugh." I put my arm around Cassidy's shoulders. "Cassidy was careful with your poster, but it fell and ripped after she turned it upside down."

Cassidy lowered her eyes. "I'll try to get you another autographed poster."

I threw my hands up in the air. "It just ripped a tiny bit in the corner, Avery. No big deal."

"No big deal to you," said Avery quietly. "But a very big deal to me."

Cassidy sucked in her breath. "Sorry."

Avery sighed. "It's okay, I guess. The rip isn't that bad. My mom told me I should frame it to protect it. She was right."

Bree spoke up. "We knew you guys pulled the prank the second we saw the room. It would have been funny if you hadn't ruined our stuff." Then she looked at the others and smiled. "Correction. It was a little funny."

The other girls smiled too!

"So you aren't mad?" I asked.

The Core Four raised their eyebrows and snorted.

"We don't get mad," said Jaelyn.

"That's good," I said.

"We get even," said Esha.

"Oh, that's bad," I said.

Jaelyn said, "When you least expect it . . ."

"Expect it," said Carly.

Why is she always popping up?

"Carly! Mind your own business," I said.

She put her nose in the air and turned to face the Core Four. "I can help you prank these girls. I have a lot of great ideas."

I thought of her wiggly worm and Gertie. I shuddered.

Esha patted her on the back. "No thanks, shrimp-o. You're just a little kid."

Carly stood tall. "I grew four inches over the winter."

Bree hugged her. "Sorry, Carly."

She flared her nostrils. "Fine." She spun around on the heel of her boot and stormed off.

Then the Core Four waved good-bye.

"Remember," said Avery. "When you least expect it . . ."

"Expect it," I whispered.

"What do you think they'll do?" asked Cassidy at dinner.

"Maybe they'll flip our stuff around," said Khadija.

"Nah," I said. "That would be lame."

"What would be lame?" asked Aunt Jane.

I waved at her. "Aw, nothing."

She shook her car keys in the air. "If I'm not back in time for the campfire, Layla's in charge.

Tell Avery and Bree that she has the music." She glanced around the room. "I'd tell them myself but I don't see them." She looked at the clock. "I'm getting some foil and plastic wrap at the store. Chef Piper said we're out and that she can't run a kitchen without it." She waved good-bye and dashed across the Pavilion.

Ryleigh rocked back and forth. "I hate not knowing when the prank's going to happen."

But we didn't have to wait long to find out.

After the campfire, we walked back to our cabin. Ryleigh opened the screen door and stopped. "Um, I think the Core Four just got even with us . . ."

I peeked inside and smiled. "Now we know why Chef Piper needed more plastic wrap and foil."

Everything in our cabin was covered with the stuff! Everything!

"Look at the beds," said Ryleigh as she tugged

at the mattresses and pillows. "They're wrapped so tight we'll need scissors to cut the stuff off. But I gotta say, this is impressive."

I went into the bathroom. My toothbrush had at least twenty layers of plastic wrap around it. Even the bar of soap was covered in plastic! The towels looked like one big piece of tinfoil!

When I saw the toilet, I laughed. It was wrapped in a combination of plastic and foil.

Funny but gross!

Khadija picked up her plant. "They actually cut foil into itty bitty strips and wrapped the stem and leaves."

She frowned as she peeled the foil off each leaf and rolled it into a little ball. "They bruised some of the leaves." She tossed the ball into the garbage can but it bounced off. It was covered in plastic, too.

Our shoes were neatly wrapped in foil like Christmas presents. Even our bathrobes hanging behind the bathroom door were wrapped in plastic.

"They look like my dad's shirts when they come back from the cleaners," said Ryleigh.

"How did they do this so fast?" asked Khadija. Then her eyes lit up. "Now we know why they took turns leaving the campfire!"

I picked up a picture frame off the desk and started to unwind it. That's when I noticed the bag of peppermint candy. Each piece was wrapped in foil!

We spent the next two hours taking off all of the foil and plastic . . . and plotting our revenge!

No one could out-prank the Four Horseketeers!

Or could they?

"Anyone have any extra foil?" asked Avery at breakfast the next day.

I yawned. "Ha, ha! Good prank. But not as good as ours."

Esha's eyes grew wide. "Are you kiddin'? Our prank was way better than yours. It probably took you all night to unwrap everything."

"Not all night," said Ryleigh. "Just half of it!"

Word of the two pranks spread across the Pavilion. Layla gave us a thumbs-up when she walked by. "I turned everything in my friends' cabin upside down too." She gave each one of us a high five. "Best prank ever."

I glanced at the Core Four. "Thanks, Layla. It was the best prank EVER."

But then Chef Piper congratulated the Core Four. "As much as I needed the wrap and foil, your prank was clever." She turned to us. "I wish I could have seen your faces when you saw your underwear wrapped in tinfoil."

Avery's face brightened. "Thanks, Chef Piper! It was designed by yours truly."

"Oh, please," I said. "I've seen that prank done in movies. Not original at all. Ours was way more original."

That's when we started arguing!

Finally, Avery covered her ears. "I hate arguing. Let's agree that both pranks were funny."

"Ours was funnier," I said. "I'm just telling it like it is."

Bree looked around the room. "Let's ask everyone here which prank was better. Then it'll be settled once and for all."

We walked around the room and told

everyone about the pranks. Everyone had an opinion.

Half of the Pony Girls said our prank was the best and half said the Core Four's was better.

"Let's keep track of the votes," said Avery as she drew some tally marks on a napkin. "You have five votes. We have seven."

Esha patted me on the back. "Face facts. Our cabin's goin' down in Storm Cliff Stables history as pullin' the best prank of the summer."

Not if I could help it!

"What do you think, Aunt Jane?" I asked.

She put down her toast and held her hands up in the air. "Oh no you don't. I'm not getting involved in this. I'm sure you girls can figure things out on your own."

"So we can't count on your vote?" I asked.

"'Fraid not," she said.

"Everyone voted then," I said. "Let's see who won bragging rights."

Avery and I carefully counted the votes. "Thirty-nine for us," said Avery. "And . . ." She bit her lip. "Thirty-nine votes for the Four Horseketeers."

"We're tied?" I slapped my cheeks. "After all that work?"

Khadija sighed. "Does that mean we're going to spend the rest of the summer trying to top each other?"

Bree shook her head. "I see way too many pranks in our future if we keep trying to one-up each other. Or we could settle for a tie."

"No way," I said. "What fun is that?"

"Not going to happen," said Avery.

"I have animals to take care of. I don't have time for more pranks," said Bree.

Jaelyn nodded. "I'm out."

Then Khadija and Ryleigh agreed with Jaelyn!

Esha mumbled, "Fine. We all know we're the best bunk anyway."

"Excuse me?" I said. "I'm a better jumper than Avery."

Avery's jaw dropped. "That's not true."

Ryleigh tapped her chin. "My vaulting routine is stronger than yours, Esha."

"Says who?" said Esha. "I've landed my dismount every time. Didn't you fall last week?"

"Says me," Ryleigh snapped back. She put her hands on her hips. "I don't remember falling last week. Sure it wasn't you?"

"Quiet down!" I hissed.

But no one was listening to anyone. Everyone was just trying to talk louder than the person next to them.

Aunt Jane glanced over at us. I smiled and waved. I figured we had about twenty seconds before she'd walk over to make sure everything was okay.

I had to prove once and for all that *we* were the prank champs. That's when I had an idea.

"Let's have a competition to see who's really the best cabin here. We could call it the Battle of the Bunks."

The arguing stopped.

"Keep talkin'," said Esha.

"We could settle this with mounted games," I said. "Think about it! You need to be a good athlete and have great riding skills and super coordination. We'd all be pretty even starting out so it would be fair, wouldn't it?"

No one said anything right away.

"We've all played the games before," I reminded them. "It will be fair and square."

Cassidy slowly raised her hand. "Um ... what exactly are mounted games?"

"Games on horseback," said Ryleigh. "Competitive games on horseback."

Avery's eyes lit up. "They combine English riding skills, which is what we're mostly trained in, with Western riding skills thrown in." She sighed. "I miss my Western riding days!"

"They're timed races," said Ryleigh. "It used to be that only Pony Clubs played the games but now everyone plays."

I nodded. "The Pony Club girls aren't too competitive. At least not around here. But I saw some grown-ups compete last year and it was intense! The team that won was going on to compete internationally."

Everyone started talking at once again.

I turned to Cassidy. "Some people call it gymkhana. Our Pony Girls have played lots of the games. That's why you see those poles and barrels set up over in the outside arena."

Bree smiled. "I used to love barrel racing. I was pretty good at it too."

"Barrel racing is my favorite game," said Khadija. "And four flag and hug the mug."

"My stable back home doesn't call it gymkhana," said Esha. "They call it O-Mok-

See. It means 'games on horseback.' My ridin' instructor said O-Mok-See is a Native American phrase."

The more we talked about it, the more excited we got.

"There's just one little problem," said Cassidy. "I just started to ride. And Bree doesn't ride at all."

Bree shrugged. "The Battle of the Bunks doesn't just have to be mounted games. We could bake cupcakes and everyone can vote for their favorite."

Everyone loved that idea!

Within ten minutes, the plan was set. We'd each picked one mounted game we wanted to play and Cassidy and Bree decided on the cupcake they wanted to bake. Each competition would be worth ten points. The team with the most points at the end would get all the bragging rights for Best Prank Ever and Best Bunk.

"Just remember," I said. "Each team is responsible for setting up your games and getting the supplies. We'll set up in back of the large arena and you girls can set up in front of the outdoor one. Does everyone agree?"

"You need to ask Aunt Jane first," said Carly.

I peeked under the table. "How long have you been under there?"

She crawled out. "She'll say yes but you still need permission."

"Scram," I said. "No little kids allowed."

She stuck her tongue out and pranced away.

"She's right," I said. "How about we both practice our own games until lunchtime and then we'll practice the other team's games?"

"Perfect," said Avery. "Everyone agree?"

Every head bobbed up and down.

"This is going to be a blast," I said as I picked up my glass of juice and raised it in the air. "No more pranks?"

Everyone chimed in. "No more pranks."

We clinked our glasses together.

"May the best bunk win!" I said.

This was gonna be easy peasy lemon squeezy!

After we got permission, we jumped into action.

I looked over our list.

1 – Barrel Racing
2 – Balloon Burst
3 – Four Flag

"Aunt Jane said a lot of these supplies are in the shed behind the Green Canteen," I said.

"Except for the barrels. They're already set up for the Pony Girls."

"What should I do?" asked Cassidy. "Should I ask Chef Piper if I can bake my cupcakes now?"

Bree walked over. "Want to make a sign for

the Battle of the Bunks? Then after that we can make our cupcakes."

Cassidy waved good-bye to us. "Let the competition begin!"

I grabbed her arm before she left. "Just don't be too friendly with the competition. Got it?"

But she didn't get it! She just laughed and walked away with Bree.

We spent the next hour setting up our games.

First we pulled the large easel and the balloons out of the shed. "We'll practice without balloons today," I said. "We don't have a lot of extras."

Khadija peeked behind a set of cones. "Here are some jousts that we can use to pop them."

"The ends aren't that sharp," I said as I touched one. "But sharp enough to pop balloons."

Then we pulled out the cones and flags.

"Lucky for us that we don't have to set up the barrels," I said.

Ryleigh took a deep breath. "I have a confession. I've never done any barrel racing before. I have no clue what to do."

I kicked the dirt. "Really? If I had known that, I would have picked another game."

Ryleigh let out a small sigh. "Just tell me what to do and I'll nail it."

I pointed to the barrels in the field. "There are three barrels that we use. The first two are across from each other and 90 feet apart." I pointed to the one farthest away. "That third barrel over there is 105 feet away from the first two. They form a triangle. See it?"

Ryleigh nodded. "Easy so far. But what do I need to do?"

"You have to enter the path from a line all the way back there," I said as I pointed behind us. "We'll have to use our boots to make a little ditch so we can see where to start and where to end. When you start the race, you can either go left or right into the first barrel. It's up to the rider."

"I'll go right," said Ryleigh.

"Okay then. Pretend I'm the horse," I said as I headed right toward the first barrel. "I have to go around the first barrel and then head over to the second barrel just like this."

I walked quickly and added some neighing for sound effects.

"Sit deep in the saddle when you make your turns. Hopefully, your horse will stay really close to the barrel. The closer they are to it, the faster your time."

I headed toward the second barrel. "Now go toward the second barrel. Go around it in the opposite direction. Then go toward the third barrel and make sure you go around it the same way you did for the second barrel. Once you go around it, you head straight for the finish line which is exactly where you started."

I zoomed to the finish line.

"Looks easy," said Ryleigh. "How do you win?"

"Whoever has the fastest time is the winner," said Khadija. "But if you can't control your horse, you won't win. One time, I was disqualified because my horse ran right past a barrel."

I groaned. "Don't do that tomorrow! We're adding up all of our times. Whichever team has the lowest score wins the event."

"I almost forgot," said Khadija. "If you or your horse hits a barrel and knocks it over, you get five seconds added on to your score." She unwrapped her head scarf and repinned it. "That happens to me a lot."

"I thought you said barrel racing was your favorite game!" I said.

"It is," said Khadija. "I'm just not very good at it."

I groaned again. "Just be sure to lean into the turns. You have to lead Butterscotch, Ryleigh. Don't let her try to lead you."

We practiced running through the cloverleaf pattern three more times until Ryleigh memorized which way to go. And when we brought our horses to the course to practice, she did great!

"You almost beat my score," I said.

I had 41 seconds. She had 51 seconds and Khadija had 103 seconds.

"You beat mine," said Khadija. She whispered something into Silver Moon's ear. Silver Moon nickered. "I told her that it was my fault we were so slow."

"Keep your legs closer to her sides," I said.

So Khadija practiced again.

When she dismounted, she beamed. "I kept my legs much, much closer this time, didn't I?"

"But you hit all three barrels," I said. "You scored 118 seconds! We'll never win with that kind of score."

All of our horses started to whinny.

I reached up and patted Minka's nose. "Do what you did today and we can beat our time." Her ears were relaxed as she bobbed her head up and down. "I think she understands me."

For the rest of our practice time, we played four flag and balloon burst.

Aunt Jane stopped by.

"Looking good, girls," said Aunt Jane. "I wanted to wish you luck."

"So you want us to win?" I asked.

She clucked her tongue. "Well, I'm wishing both teams good luck. I don't care who wins as long as everyone has fun and plays fair and square."

She walked around the cloverleaf pattern. "I used to love barrel racing. I was pretty good back in the day. I once hit two barrels but still won the competition."

"Want to trade places with me?" said Khadija. "I'm not very good at it."

Aunt Jane rubbed her back. "But do you have fun racing?"

"As long as Ainsley doesn't yell at her," said Ryleigh.

I batted my eyelashes. "Me? Yell? You must have me confused with someone else."

Aunt Jane pulled my helmet down over my eyes. "No yelling, Ainsley. This is a friendly competition." She pulled a stopwatch out of her pocket. "Just to be fair, I'm going to time all the events. This way, no one can accuse anyone of cheating or not keeping accurate time. My time is the official time. Are we all in agreement?"

"Fine with me," said Khadija.

Ryleigh gave Aunt Jane a thumbs-up.

"Are you sure you know how to use that thing?" I asked. "I have a timer in my cabin that's easy to use."

Aunt Jane rolled her eyes. "Trust me, Ainsley. I've been the official timekeeper here ever since

I opened this camp. Never had a problem before and I don't expect to have one tomorrow."

I threw my hands up in the air. "Then I guess I'm fine with it, too."

Aunt Jane pulled a little container out of her other pocket. "Breath mint before lunch anyone?"

She shook one into Khadija's hand then Ryleigh's hand. They popped them into their mouths and started walking toward the Pavilion. Then I held out my hand. But when I popped it into my mouth, I almost gagged.

Gross. "This doesn't taste like mint!"

"It's mint and ginger," said Aunt Jane and she took the horses' lead ropes and started to walk back to the stable.

"I need to brush my teeth," I said. "I can't stand the taste."

So while Khadija and Ryleigh walked to the Pavilion, I ran back to the cabin.

Esha was standing right in front of our cabin. "How was practice?"

"Great," I said. "We're going to win the whole thing."

"Not if I can help it," she yelled out as I ran into my cabin.

I headed straight for the bathroom and smiled when I noticed the bar of soap still wrapped in tinfoil.

The Core Four did pull off a good prank.

I grabbed my toothbrush and toothpaste and brushed, brushed, brushed!

Then I looked in the mirror and screamed when I saw what was staring back at me!

I marched straight out the cabin door and stormed into the Pavilion. I rushed over to where everyone was sitting and lowered my head.

"You lied," I mumbled to the Core Four.

Khadija leaned over. "We can't hear you, Ainsley. What did you say?"

I took a deep breath. "I said you lied. You said no more pranks."

The Core Four were great actresses. They pretended they had no idea what I was talking about.

"What do you mean?" asked Esha.

I parted my lips so they could see my teeth.

Everyone gasped.

Except Esha.

She laughed so hard that she fell out of her seat.

Cassidy moved in for a closer look. "Blue teeth? What happened?"

"I was pranked! One of *them* put blue food coloring in my toothpaste. I wasn't paying attention and just squeezed it out and brushed." I clenched my jaw and let them have another look.

Now everyone laughed just as hard as Esha.

"It's not funny," I said. "I have blue teeth!" I shook my fist in the air. "Which one of you did this?"

Avery leaned back in her chair. "Not me."

"Me either," said Bree.

Jaelyn tried to stop laughing but couldn't. "It wasn't me. But it's an awesome prank!"

I glared at Esha.

"Don't be lookin' at me," she said.

"It was you, Esha," I snapped. "Admit it. You're always clowning around. Pulling pranks."

"Not this time," she said.

I poked my finger into her chest. "It was you. I just saw you standing outside our cabin."

She backed away. "But I have to pass by your cabin to get to the Pavilion so you can't blame it on me. Lots of people walk by your cabin."

"Someone's lying," I said. "I'll figure out who it is."

I sat down. I knew it was Esha! Somehow, I would figure out a way to prove it.

I slouched down in my seat and wished I could not talk to anyone until we went to afternoon practice.

I looked at Ryleigh and crossed my fingers. "I like the mounted games the Core Four picked out," I said. "Have you ever competed in pole bending, the pony express, or lucky ducky?"

"Yep," she said. "All three."

I let out a sigh of relief. *Whew!* Until Khadija spoke up.

"I hate to tell you this, Ainsley, but I've never competed in pole bending before. Honestly, I've never even seen anyone do it."

I rubbed my temples. Back to square one.

That's when Khadija and Ryleigh burst out laughing.

"Sorry," said Khadija. "It's just that you look funny with blue teeth."

Ryleigh tried to stop laughing but her lips kept quivering. "It'll wear off soon. Just drink a lot of water and try brushing your teeth with real toothpaste next time."

I sneered at them. "Thanks for the tips. I need to think of a prank to pull on Esha."

Khadija sighed. "She said she didn't do it."

"She's lying," I said. "Who else could it be?"

"But we promised we wouldn't keep on pranking each other," said Ryleigh. "So just drop it, okay?"

"Esha promised too," I said. "Did she drop it?"

Ryleigh narrowed her eyes. "If Aunt Jane knows you're fighting with Esha, she'll cancel the Battle of the Bunks. Can't you worry about pulling a prank on her after the competition?"

Khadija agreed. "Besides, we need to practice these three games if we want to win."

I hopped up. "Oh, I wanna win alright. I wanna win bad!"

Focus, I told myself. *Worry about Esha later.*

"Okay, Khadija, about pole bending . . ." I counted the poles. "There are always six poles. Each one is supposed to be twenty-one feet from the others." I pointed to the base. "The poles are usually six feet high and the base can't be more than fourteen inches wide."

Khadija inspected the base. "Makes sense. You don't want it to interfere with the horse's hooves."

"Exactly," I said. "The rules are a lot like barrel racing. You can start by either going to the left or to the right of the poles. But instead of a cloverleaf pattern, you have to weave through the poles like a snake."

"A serpentine pattern?" asked Khadija.

I nodded. "If you knock over the pole, five seconds gets added to your time. If you miss one of the turns, you're disqualified."

"Just like in barrel racing," said Ryleigh.

I found the starting line the girls had made. "We start here. Don't forget to look ahead to where you want to go. Use your legs to help your horse go in the right direction. Lean forward as you go into the poles."

"How long does it take to go through them?" asked Khadija.

I scratched my head. "I knew someone who ran it in twenty-four seconds. That's speedy quick. My lowest time was twenty-nine seconds. I want to break twenty-six seconds this time."

"Think we should practice with the horses?" asked Ryleigh.

"We better," I said. "If we want to win." I hopped around on one foot. "But before I get

Minka, I'm going to run back to the cabin. I need to go to the bathroom."

When I got back with Minka, Ryleigh and Khadija were already running through the poles. Ryleigh and Butterscotch were zooming through the course, but Khadija and Silver Moon seemed to run in slow motion.

"What took you so long?" asked Khadija when she crossed the finish line. "You've been gone forever."

Minka greeted each horse with a low neigh. Then she hung her head over Silver Moon's neck and hugged her. They both nickered until Butterscotch joined them.

"I had to go to the bathroom," I said. "Remember?"

"For twenty minutes?" asked Ryleigh.

I flared my nostrils. "I had a pain in my stomach but it's gone now."

"Butterscotch wants a hug, too," said Ryleigh.

Minka lifted her head and swung it over in Butterscotch's direction. They rubbed their noses together.

"True friends," said Khadija. "Just like us."

I mounted Minka and brought her back to the start line. For the next hour, we competed against each other in pole bending, the pony express, and lucky ducky. I won all three games every time we ran the courses.

"You're good," said Khadija.

"You're not," I said.

Ryleigh shook her head. "That's not nice, Ainsley."

"You know me," I said. "I just tell it like it is . . . But . . . I didn't finish."

Khadija tilted her head. "Go ahead."

"I was going to say you're not too good at barrel racing but you're really a good competitor when it comes to these games."

Her face lit up. "Thanks!"

"I'm hot," I said. "And sticky. I want a shower."

Ryleigh sniffed the air. "You need a shower. We all need one."

So after we dropped off the horses in the pasture, we went inside our cabin. Cassidy was writing a letter to her grandmother. She filled us in on her cupcake making and we filled her in on the mounted games.

"Sounds like fun," I said. "We . . ."

But I didn't finish my sentence because the Core Four barged into the room.

"You promised no more pranks," said Bree.

"We kept our promise," I said. I flashed them my teeth. "Unlike someone in your cabin."

"Then how do you explain this?" said Avery.

She untied her robe and let it drop to the floor. She had on a green bathing suit.

"Explain what?" I asked.

When she turned around, she revealed a completely purple back!

"What happened to you?" asked Khadija. "What is that stuff?"

Avery picked her robe up and put it back on. "Like you guys don't know!"

"I don't know," said Cassidy. "Honest."

"Neither do I," said Ryleigh.

Khadija shrugged. "Don't look at me."

"Me either," I said. "Tell us what it is."

"Grape juice," said Avery. Then she paused. "Actually, the powdered mix for the grape juice."

"How did it get on your back?" I asked.

Avery folded her arms. "One of you unscrewed the nozzle in our shower and scooped some of the powdered mix into it. When I turned on the water, the powdered mix turned to grape juice and sprayed all over me." She pulled her robe tighter. "I'm glad my back was toward the nozzle and not my face."

We laughed.

"It's not funny," said Jaelyn. "What if it would

have stained her face?"

I pointed to my mouth. "Like the blue food coloring stained my teeth?"

"So did you do it to get even?" asked Avery.

I shook my head. "No way. I didn't do it. When would I have had time to pull a prank like that? I was practicing for tomorrow all afternoon with Ryleigh and Khadija."

"That's not true," said Esha. "You came back here. By yourself."

"No, I didn't," I said.

Khadija and Ryleigh gave me a weird look.

"Oh . . . I forgot about that," I said. "I came back to use the bathroom."

"Our bathroom?" asked Jaelyn. She huffed and puffed her cheeks.

"Why would I use your bathroom when mine is right next door?" I asked. "I went to the bathroom and then went back to practice."

I could tell the Core Four didn't believe me.

"Remember," said Avery. "We don't get mad. We get even."

When they left, my bunkmates surrounded me. They looked worried.

"You shouldn't have done that," said Khadija.

"You said no more pranks," said Ryleigh.

Cassidy shook her head. "A promise is supposed to be a promise, you know."

Great! Not only did the Core Four not believe me, but even my own bunkmates thought I was lying.

Chapter 6

A Cupcake Disaster

We avoided the Core Four at the campfire that night and they avoided us, too.

When they performed their skit, I didn't clap for them. Khadija did until I flashed my teeth and gave her the evil eye.

"No clapping for liars," I said.

Esha overheard me. "You're the ones who pulled a prank on Avery today. You broke your promise."

Avery sat directly in front of me. I could see a dark purple stain under her ponytail.

"Liar, liar, pants on fire," I whispered.

Aunt Jane spoke after the skits were over. "Welcome to another wonderful campfire. Thanks to Cabins 16, 4, and 11 today for such awesome skits. But, I'm sorry to inform you that there won't be any s'mores tonight."

Everyone moaned and groaned.

Aunt Jane held up her hand. "I accidently left the chocolate bars and marshmallows in my car today. They're a gooey, icky mess, but I have an alternative plan."

Everyone cheered.

"I'm sure by now you've all heard about the Battle of the Bunks competition tomorrow. I expect everyone to be dressed and eating by eight o'clock. The games begin at nine o'clock sharp. The girls agreed that whoever wins gets full bragging rights." She looked a little confused. "To what, I'm not sure. But I like that the girls are working out some issues themselves."

Some of the girls started chanting, "Go Core Four! Go Core Four! Go Core Four!

No one chanted our names, so I started the chant myself. "Go Horseketeers! Go Horseketeers!

Go Horseketeers!" By the time I said it for the third time, a lot of other campers were chanting with me.

After a minute, Aunt Jane asked everyone to stop.

"Part of the competition is a baking competition. You were going to taste both cupcakes tomorrow after dinner and vote for your favorites then. But since we don't have our usual campfire treat, you'll taste and vote now."

The place erupted. "Cupcakes! Cupcakes! Cupcakes!"

Layla walked over to the picnic table and put two large boxes on it. She lifted the lid to reveal Cassidy's and Bree's cupcakes.

"Girls," said Aunt Jane. "Could you come up and describe your cupcakes? Let us know what we're about to eat."

Cassidy bounced out of her seat and shuffled over to the table. She grabbed one of her cupcakes. "This is my version of a s'mores cupcake. It's chocolate cake with marshmallow frosting. I sprinkled bits of graham crackers on top of each one."

Everyone clapped. Cassidy bowed and flashed the peace sign to the crowd.

Then Bree went up and waved her cupcake in the air. "I made a lemon cupcake with a surprise filling inside. I'll give you a hint. It's fruity! Then I used a lemon frosting and made a horseshoe decoration out of fondant and put it on top."

The clapping erupted again.

Bree blew kisses to the crowd.

"You're going to taste both of them," said Aunt Jane. "But you're voting for only one. Whoever gets the most votes scores ten points for their team in the Battle of the Bunks. Remember, you're not voting for the girl. You're voting for the cupcake."

Layla yelled out, "Come and get 'em!"

Everyone rushed toward the table, but I wished Cassidy good luck first.

"You got this, Cassidy! Everyone loves chocolate and s'mores." I pointed to the table. "Look how everyone's crowded around your box." I licked my lips. "You're going to earn us the first ten points in the competition."

Cassidy beamed as she jumped up and down. "I hope so! I can't wait to eat one, too. I wasn't sure if I made enough so I didn't get to have one yet. I hope there's one left for me."

Then her smile faded. She stopped jumping. Her lips curled and her nose crinkled. "Hey! That girl just bit into my cupcake and spit it out into the fire."

I turned around to see three other girls doing the same thing. Then four. Then five . . . six . . .

What was going on?

Cassidy confronted them. "Why are you spitting out my cupcake?"

Lexi, a first-year camper, shook her head. "It tastes yucky."

Carly scrunched her nose. "It tastes . . . salty."

Cassidy gasped. "Salty? There's hardly any salt in this recipe."

Carly held out one of the cupcakes. "Try it."

Everywhere I looked, girls were spitting out Cassidy's cupcake. I even saw Aunt Jane toss hers in the trash can.

Cassidy took the cupcake from Carly and bit into it. She chewed it for a second before shaking her head. "It's salty, all right. Gross!" She tossed it straight into the fire.

I couldn't believe it could taste that bad so I took a little nibble.

"You shouldn't have done that," said Carly. "We told you it wasn't any good."

I spit it out. "It's like eating a shaker of salt."

I glanced over at Bree's cupcakes. There was only one left. She was sharing her secret filling

recipe with a group of girls. Then I saw Layla swipe the last cupcake out of Bree's box.

"You blew it, Cassidy," I said. "What went wrong?"

Khadija walked up carrying Bree's cupcake. "These are so tasty!"

Cassidy and I both put our hands on our hips.

"Really, Khadija?" I said. "Supporting the enemy?"

"I'm not voting for it," said Khadija. "Don't worry."

"You may as well," said Cassidy. "Everyone else will." She wiped her eyes. "I have no idea why my cupcake tastes like salt."

"Because you obviously used salt, Cass!" I said. "It's not rocket science."

Cassidy slapped her cheeks. "Oh no! I must have scooped salt out of the canister instead of sugar. What a stupid mistake."

"That can't be it," said Chef Piper. "We don't have a canister filled with salt. Sugar? Yes. Flour? Yes. But salt? Nope. I keep the salt in the pantry. Not near the baking station."

Cassidy blinked hard.

"Well then how did the salt get inside these cupcakes?" I asked.

Chef Piper scratched her head. "I'm not sure. Did you go back to the pantry and get the sack of salt?"

"Nope. I needed two cups of sugar," said Cassidy. "So I took the lid off of the canister and spooned out the right amount."

"Are you sure that's what you did?" I asked. "You're sure it was the sugar canister?"

"If you spell sugar S-U-G-A-R than I am positive that's the one I used," she said. "I've made this recipe at least a dozen times and I've never had this problem."

I saw Aunt Jane collecting ballots. I dragged Cassidy over to her. "You can't count these votes. It's not fair."

"Why isn't it fair?" asked Aunt Jane. "Cassidy and Bree presented their cupcakes. The girls ate both and then voted."

Cassidy's voice cracked when she spoke. "Did you taste mine, Aunt Jane? It was terrible."

Aunt Jane put her arm around her. "I think you might have gotten some of the ingredients mixed up."

"Which is why you shouldn't count the votes," I said.

Avery overheard. "Sorry, Cassidy. I've eaten your cupcakes before. They're usually awesome. But fair is fair. This was a contest." She pointed to the ballots in Aunt Jane's hand. "The girls voted."

"But . . ." I started to say.

Aunt Jane shut me down. "The votes count."

A few minutes later, Aunt Jane read the results. "With a vote of 58 to 6, the winner is . . . Bree."

The Core Four chest bumped each other.

"At least I got six votes," said Cassidy. "The Four Horseketeers and two others. I wonder who else voted for me."

I shrugged. "No idea."

I didn't have the heart to tell her that I voted for her three times.

No one felt much like talking after the campfire.

"Let's get to bed early," I said. "We have a big day tomorrow."

Cassidy sniffled. "We're already ten points behind. I just don't get it. I'm 100 percent positive I used sugar."

Ryleigh handed Cassidy a tissue. "You think you added sugar. But we know it was actually salt. Do you think . . . ?"

She stopped talking.

"Do you think what?" I asked. "Spill it."

"I don't want to start any trouble," said Ryleigh. "But . . ."

I sat up in my bunk. "But what?"

"Do you think someone could have switched out the sugar and put salt in the canister instead?" asked Ryleigh.

Cassidy and Khadija shot straight up in their bunks.

"You mean like a prank?" I asked. "Another prank?"

Cassidy hopped out of bed. "That makes perfect sense. Someone had to have messed with my recipe. Honestly, I was the only one in the kitchen except for Chef Piper. She checked in with me a few times."

"Maybe someone knew you were going into the kitchen to make cupcakes at that exact time. Think about it. The person could have gone in a few minutes before you did and swapped out the sugar for salt."

"Who would do that?"

I had a stinking suspicion.

Esha!

"Bree was the only one who knew I was making cupcakes at that time," said Cassidy. "And Chef Piper, of course."

"Chef Piper would never do it," I said. "She'd get fired from her job."

Everyone agreed.

"Bree had the chance to pull the prank but that's just not something Bree would do," I said. "She's one of the nicest girls at camp."

Again, everyone agreed.

"Could it be the same person who put blue food coloring in the toothpaste?" I said.

Khadija whined. "The pranks have to stop. They're starting to cause real problems between friends." She got out of her bed and sat on the bottom of mine. "No more pranks, Ainsley. I bet that grape juice stain will be on Avery's back for days and days. I hope Aunt Jane doesn't see it. Or her mom."

"I had nothing to do with that prank," I said.

"I told you guys before that I didn't do it. Do I think it was a funny prank? Yes. Do I wish that I had thought of it? Yep. But to be honest, if I did pull off a prank like that, I'd want people to know. Bragging rights, for sure."

I pulled the covers under my chin. "I think I know who did all of the pranks. The grape juice, the toothpaste, and the salt."

"Who?" said everyone at the same time.

"Esha!" I said. "It's such an Esha thing to do, isn't it?"

Cassidy shrugged. "I don't really know her too well."

"We've known her for four years," I said. "Remember the prank she pulled last summer about that ghost from a village outside of Mumbai? What was his name?"

"Suraj!" said Khadija. "He was a poor boy from a village that had a famous riding academy. But only the rich people could afford to take riding lessons there. He stole a horse and planned on selling it so he'd have enough money to take lessons."

"Then what happened?" asked Cassidy.

I shrugged. "It doesn't really matter. But I remember what happened at camp after she told us the story. Things started disappearing. She tried to convince everyone that it was the ghost of Suraj who was stealing from us. She had a lot of us fooled. She said herself how no one could pull off a better prank than she could."

"But what about the grape drink mix?" asked Cassidy. "Wouldn't she have put the mix into *our* shower head?"

"Unless she wanted to throw us off," I said. "I think she did it. And I think she's laughing at all of us right now."

Khadija wasn't so sure.

"I don't think so, Ainsley. She'd never do something like that to Avery."

"Something like what?" I said. "It's just juice. Nothing harmful. Just a stupid prank. Not a big deal."

Ryleigh yawned. "The more I think about it, the more I think you could be right, Ainsley."

"Me too," said Cassidy.

"Good night," said Khadija as she rolled over. "We have a big day tomorrow."

But I couldn't sleep. I tossed and turned all night. Finally, at five o'clock, I got up and figured I'd help Bree with some chores or spend time with Minka in the stable.

I crept out of bed and threw on my jeans and sweatshirt. Since I was going to the stable, I grabbed my helmet and put it on.

When I stepped outside, I was surprised how quiet and peaceful camp was. All the cabins were still dark, including Aunt Jane's and Layla's.

I walked down to the stable and peeked inside. I saw a coffee mug on a table but no one was around. I walked down to Minka's stall.

"Hiya, girl," I whispered. "Good morning." I kissed her nose and scratched her belly. Her ears were bent forward. "You're a good girl. Alert so early in the morning." She swished her tail as I scratched her belly a little harder. "No one believes me that your tail swishing means you're happy, Minka. But I see when you swish it. I don't care what the books say. I know it's how you talk to me."

Then Minka let out the sweetest neigh. It made my heart melt. "You're the most beautiful horse at Storm Cliff Stables." She swished her tail again. "I meant to say in the whole world."

Swish swish.

I leaned in and whispered, "I don't want to make the other horses jealous, but I brought you a peppermint." I pulled it out of my pocket and smiled when I realized it was still wrapped in foil. I peeled it off and placed it in the palm of my hand. I made sure my fingers were pulled in tight along with my thumb. I stiffened my hand and placed it about five inches under Minka's chin. She bent her neck down and brushed her fuzzy lips against my hand. "Lap it up, girl. If we win today, you'll get another mint. Deal?"

After making sure her water and feed buckets were cleaned and filled, I gave her another hug.

"Even if we don't win, I'm still giving you another mint."

Swish swish.

As I left the stable, the sky was just starting to get a little lighter. I could make out the shapes of the barn, the cabins, the Green Canteen, the fences, and the Pavilion. Except for the Pavilion and the soft glow of a few lamps in the stable, Storm Cliff Stables was still pretty much asleep.

Halfway back to the cabin, I turned in the opposite direction and walked toward the Pavilion. My stomach was growling and I hoped I could get a bowl of cereal. I slipped in through a side door and walked into the dining hall. It was dark and quiet.

Too dark. Too quiet.

I heard someone humming in the kitchen. I poked my head inside the kitchen door.

"Chef Piper?" I called out.

No answer.

"Anyone in here?" I said a little louder.

No answer.

Then I heard something crash to the ground in the pantry.

I walked toward the pantry door and swung it open.

But I didn't find Chef Piper inside.

I found Esha instead.

"Esha? What are you doing here?"

But when I saw the sack of salt in her hands, I already knew the answer.

Chapter 8

Let the Games Begin

Esha grimaced when she saw me. "It's not what you think, Ainsley."

I looked her up and down. "Really? Because to me, it looks like you got caught with a sack of *salt* in your hand. Salt that was mysteriously dumped into cupcakes yesterday."

She brushed past me and dropped the sack on the table. "I couldn't sleep. I'm way too excited about today. So I came in here early to get somethin' to eat. Honestly, I was hopin' to find some donuts that I could take back to my cabin. When I went into the pantry and saw the salt, I got to thinkin' about those cupcakes."

She stuck out her tongue and pretended she was throwing up. "I'm just as curious as you are to find out how that salt got in the batter."

"I know how," I said.

Esha's eyes widened. "Then let me in on it."

"You did it," I said. "I'm not sure when you did it, but it has your name written all over it."

She laughed. "No way. I was just goin' to compare the salt to the sugar. To see if I could tell the difference just by lookin' at it."

"Yeah, sure," I said. "Whatever you say."

I stood there for a minute dying to get the whole scoop. To be able to tell the others that I solved the mystery right before the battle started would have been fun. But I didn't want to argue with anyone at the moment. Especially on Battle of the Bunks day. "Can we talk about this later?"

She nodded.

"But you do know I'm going to have to tell everyone what I just saw in here," I said.

She shrugged. "No one will believe you. Know why?"

"Why?"

"'Cause I'm innocent. I wasn't doing anything wrong."

I turned around and started to walk out of the kitchen. "Good luck today," I yelled over my shoulder. "You're gonna need it!"

When I got back to the cabin, I told the girls what had happened.

"Guess I was wrong," said Khadija. "But at least we know who did it. We can find out why she did it after the battle today."

After breakfast, everyone headed over to the outdoor arena. There was a huge sign that said Battle of the Bunks. It was at least twenty feet long and was staked into the ground.

"Look at that sign!" I said. "You and Bree did a great job, Cass."

Cassidy looked nervous. "I hope it doesn't fall down."

After Aunt Jane introduced us and our horses,

we started the competition.

"Barrel races are always fun, campers," said Aunt Jane. "You need to have good speed and agility and be able to control your horse through the turns. The Four Horseketeers are going first."

We mounted our horses and trotted behind the start line that we had made in the dirt.

When Aunt Jane lowered the flag, Ryleigh headed left toward the first barrel. She zipped around the cloverleaf in no time and crossed the finish line is thirty-four seconds.

I gave her a high five. "You kept Butterscotch close to the barrels. Awesome job."

Khadija's time was a lot higher because she hit all three barrels.

I had a flawless run. Best ever! I didn't hit any barrels and Minka was so close to the barrels that I could almost feel them. I was feeling pretty good about our scores until Avery mounted her horse. Then something odd happened. She hit all three barrels, too. Just like Khadija. And her timing was off. It was almost like she and Sapphire were racing in slow motion. Esha and Jaelyn had much better times even though they each hit a barrel, too.

Layla read the results. "Remember, the Core Four are already on the board for last night's cupcake win." She cleared her throat. "The first round goes to . . . the Four Horseketeers, who won

this round by a whopping thirty-seven seconds."

Everyone clapped for us. Even the Core Four! Layla recorded the totals on a chalkboard.

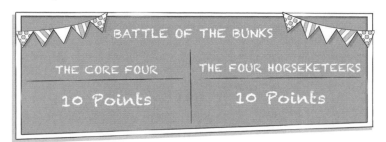

BATTLE OF THE BUNKS

THE CORE FOUR	THE FOUR HORSEKETEERS
10 Points	10 Points

"We're moving on to the balloon burst. This is a timed relay race," said Aunt Jane. "The clock is set at three minutes. Each rider takes turns weaving through the barrels until they get to the balloon board. Once they're there, they use a joust to pop a balloon as they continue around the board and back to the starting line. Then rider two goes and so on.

"The girls have to work well with their horses. If the horse gallops too fast, it will be hard to pop a balloon. But if the horse moves too slow, they won't get to pop as many balloons."

This time, the Core Four went first.

Esha started off the race and easily used her joust to pop a balloon. The crowd cheered.

She got back to the finish line and handed Avery her joust. Avery and Sapphire overshot the board and lost their chance to pop a balloon. When Avery handed off the joust to Jaelyn, she almost dropped it. Jaelyn had a little trouble weaving around the second barrel, but she was able to pop a balloon.

Esha was up again. The crowd started chanting, "Esha, Esha, Esha."

She gave them a show. After she popped the balloon, she blew a kiss to the crowd.

Show-off.

The handoff from Esha to Avery was smooth, but Sapphire hit the first barrel and stopped! Avery quickly got her galloping again and was able to pop the balloon.

"She just wasted a lot of time," said Ryleigh.

And suddenly, the race was over.

"Our turn," I said. "We got this!"

I ran my hands along Minka's belly and back. "Ready, girl? Just don't overshoot the board, okay?"

We all mounted our horses and took our positions behind the line. I was going first. I adjusted my helmet and was off! Minka was a little cautious around the first barrel but handled the rest like a pro. I was easily able to pop a balloon and pass off the joust to Ryleigh.

"Look at Ryleigh go," I said to Khadija. "She and Butterscotch work so well together."

They were back super quick. Even Khadija was able to pop a balloon easily. When we finished the race, we had popped eleven balloons in three minutes!

"The Core Four popped seven balloons," said Layla. "The Four Horseketeers popped eleven! Ten points are awarded to the Four

Horseketeers!" Then she changed the score on the chalkboard.

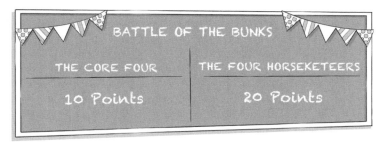

BATTLE OF THE BUNKS

THE CORE FOUR	THE FOUR HORSEKETEERS
10 Points	20 Points

"We're going to start the next competition," said Aunt Jane. "Four flag."

Layla put four flags on long poles in a cone. Then she put four cones, in colors to match the flags, around the course.

"The girls need to weave through the barrels and get to the other side," said Aunt Jane. "They must pull a flag out of the cone and go put it in its matching cone on the field. After all four flags are in the right cones, the rider must go back through the barrels and cross the finish line.

"That's when I'll stop the clock. We'll then combine all times together and the team with the lowest time will win this round."

I loved this race! I went first and was able to put all the flags in their matching cones in just forty-two seconds. Ryleigh finished the course in fifty-six seconds and Khadija only needed fifty-one seconds to cross the finish line.

"Impressive!" said Aunt Jane. "Can the Core Four get a combined time lower than 149 seconds?"

The answer was no! Jaelyn and Esha flew through the course and beat my time. I was sure we were going to lose the round once Avery raced. But she goofed. She finished the course quickly but put the orange flag in the red cone and the red flag in the orange cone. She crossed the finish line and pumped her fist up and down. She thought they had won the round.

Aunt Jane shook her head. "Rider didn't complete the course correctly. Go back and fix errors."

Avery looked confused. She thought she hadn't gone back through the barrels so she repeated that step. When she finally realized she didn't match the flags to the correct cones, it was too late. She was already over three minutes!

Layla changed the chalkboard scores.

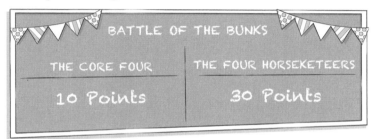

BATTLE OF THE BUNKS

THE CORE FOUR	THE FOUR HORSEKETEERS
10 Points	30 Points

Aunt Jane spoke again. "That's all for now. We need to rest and water the horses. We'll conclude the competition after our lunch this afternoon."

Cassidy rushed over to us. "We're awesome, aren't we? We're crushing them."

It was true. We were crushing them. But something didn't feel right.

Were we really that good, or were the Core Four simply that bad?

Chapter 9
The Truth Comes Out

"I can't believe we've won every game so far," said Cassidy. "We're rockin' it."

I picked the crust off of my bread and rolled it into a ball. "I can't believe how bad Avery's doing. It doesn't make sense."

Cassidy shrugged. "You're just better than she is. No big deal."

But it was a big deal. Avery's times were so off that I was actually worried.

"Do you think Sapphire's okay?" I asked.

Ryleigh nodded. "She's healthy. Dr. Samuels gave her a checkup last week."

I dropped my sandwich onto my plate. "Something's wrong with Avery today."

"Yeah, she's as slow as Khadija," said Ryleigh.

Khadija blew raspberries at Ryleigh.

"I want to win," I said, "but not if there's no real competition."

I walked over to the Core Four's table. Bree and Jaelyn were smiling but Esha and Avery looked upset.

"No braggin' allowed," said Esha. "Until you win the whole thing."

Avery bit into her apple. "*If* they win the whole thing. We have three battles left."

"Do you feel okay?" I asked Avery. "Your times are slow. I'm not trying to start trouble but . . ."

"But what?" she asked.

"I really thought our scores would be a lot closer," I said.

Avery let out a loud yawn. She covered her mouth and rubbed her eyes. "Sorry. I just haven't been sleeping lately."

"Too much worrying about the Battle of the Bunks?" I asked.

"Nah. It would be fun to win but, really, it's just a friendly competition. At least on my part." She yawned again. "I just keep finding these worms in my bunk. They're so gross and I'm totally freaking out. We think they're coming up through the floorboards."

"Worms?" I asked. "As in wiggly worms?"

She nodded. "I swear. I've been staying in that cabin for years and we've never had any worms in our cabin. If they were just in the cabin, I'd be upset. But to pull down my sheets and have them in my bunk? I'm totally freaked."

CARLY!

Now it all made sense!

"I think you've been pranked again, Avery. Those worms aren't coming up through the floorboards and getting in your bunk. Someone put them there."

Avery's mouth dropped open. "Think so? I'd feel better if it was just a prank. I could stop that.

But if they're coming up through . . ."

I grabbed her arm. "Come with me."

I led her past the milk machines, around the salad bar, and behind the dessert table. Carly was sitting alone drinking chocolate milk.

I pointed to her. "Carly is the one who's been pranking us. The blue food coloring. The whole salt incident. The powdered drink mix. And most definitely the worms."

Carly batted her eyelashes. "Me?"

By now, the rest of the Core Four and the Four Horseketeers had gathered around us.

"Her?" said Esha. "You're kiddin', aren't you? She's just a little kid."

Carly puffed out her chest. "I'm nine and a half. And little kids can do big things."

"Like pull pranks?" asked Avery.

Carly took a deep breath and then lowered her eyes. "Yeah. Like pull pranks. All of them."

Esha snapped her fingers. "Looks like I'm off

the hook! How did you figure out she was the prankster?"

"She mentioned wanting to prank Avery with worms way before the pranks started. I didn't know she actually went ahead and did it until Avery mentioned the worm problem a few minutes ago."

Carly hit the side of her head with an open palm. "I forgot about our talk! I doomed myself."

"Why did you pull all of those pranks?" I asked.

Carly slurped her milk. "Because everyone said I was too young to help out with pranks."

She got all sassy on us.

"Proved you right, didn't I?" She chugged the rest of the milk. "I thought they were funny. But I didn't know the food coloring would make your teeth that blue. And I didn't know how much salt you'd be putting in the cupcakes. Sorry about that."

"At least I know I can sleep tonight in a worm-free bed," said Avery. "I feel better already." She jogged in place. "Energized."

I flashed her my blue teeth. "I hope not too energized. I still want to win today!"

When we started the games in the afternoon, it was obvious that Avery was now in it to win it.

"Welcome to the outdoor arena," said Aunt Jane. "We're going to start this afternoon's competition with some pole bending."

By the time it was my turn, my team had a combined score of eighty-six seconds.

I scratched between Minka's ears. "Ready, girl? We're going to have to fly through this course. We're going right first. Understand?"

When Aunt Jane lowered the flag and yelled go, I squeezed my legs into Minka's sides and she took off running.

As I approached the first turn, I leaned forward. We picked up speed.

"Stay close to the pole, Minka," I whispered.

I rounded the second pole and continued the weaving pattern. Before I knew it, I had crossed the finish line.

"Time!" yelled Aunt Jane.

I dismounted and hugged Minka before heading over to Aunt Jane.

"Great time," she said. "Twenty-nine seconds."

I kicked the dirt. "That's all? That's my personal record. I wanted to beat it."

"Good job," said Avery as she mounted Sapphire. "You're the first one to have a clean run on the course. Everyone else knocked down at least one pole."

Aunt Jane asked for quiet. "Three, two, one, go!" screamed Aunt Jane as she lowered the flag.

Avery and Sapphire tore across the starting line and headed to the left side of the course. She sat deep in the saddle and I could tell by the way she moved that she used her lower body and legs much more than I did. She already looked like an Olympian.

They zigzagged through the pattern so quickly that if you sneezed, you might have missed the entire race!

"Time!" yelled Aunt Jane as they crossed the finish line.

I crossed my fingers.

"Twenty-one seconds," said Aunt Jane.

Avery beamed.

Layla added our scores together. "The Core Four's combined total for this event was 105 seconds. The Four Horseketeers came in at 115 seconds. Ten points are awarded to the Core Four."

I studied the chalkboard.

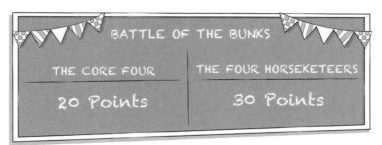

"Next up is the pony express," said Aunt Jane.

Layla and Aunt Jane quickly moved a few poles around. Bree and Cassidy grabbed burlap bags filled with letters and walked to opposite sides of the course.

"Pony Girls! Pay attention to this race," said Aunt Jane. "You'll participate in this relay style event against each other in two weeks."

Aunt Jane pointed to Bree and Cassidy.

"They're the postal workers for their teams. Each rider begins at the starting barrel and weaves through these four poles just like they did in the last race. If they knock one over, they get five seconds added to their time."

"They need to go directly across and get a letter from the mail carrier on the other side. Once they get it, they need to go back around the poles and give the letter to the next rider who is waiting behind the barrel. The clock runs until the last rider hands her letter to Layla at the ending barrel and she yells time."

Avery's team lined up.

"Esha's first," I said. "She usually knocks over a lot of poles."

I crossed my fingers as Aunt Jane lowered her flag and counted down.

Esha and Queenie took off and moved through the poles easily. She grabbed the letter from Bree and snaked her way back to Jaelyn. Jaelyn fumbled with the letter but held on to it. She zoomed through the course much faster than Esha but knocked down three poles.

"That's fifteen seconds added on to their team score," said Cassidy.

My eyes were glued to Jaelyn and Blue as she passed the letter to Avery. It was seamless. And so was Avery. Again.

Then it was our turn.

Khadija went first and although she had a clean run, she was slow through the turns.

Ryleigh looked a lot like Avery going through the course. When it was my turn, I dropped the letter and had five seconds added to my time.

We huddled around Layla waiting for the results.

"The Core Four's combined total for this event was 114 seconds. The Four Horseketeers came in at 115 seconds. Ten points awarded to the Core Four!"

We lost this round by one second! If only I hadn't dropped that letter!

While everyone clapped, I looked at the chalkboard again.

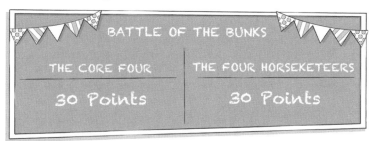

BATTLE OF THE BUNKS

THE CORE FOUR	THE FOUR HORSEKETEERS
30 Points	30 Points

"Next up," said Aunt Jane, "is lucky ducky."

I passed Carly on the way to the next event.

"Avery's racing a lot better this afternoon, huh?" She patted my back. "You shouldn't have told her about the worms, ya know."

She took the words right out of my mouth!

"Did you hear me, Ainsley?"

I leaned over to pick up a penny.

"That's good luck!" said Carly. "Make a wish."

I closed my eyes.

I wish Carly Jacobs would wiggle away.

"This is the last round," announced Aunt Jane. "Lucky ducky is a blast to play. Each player has to zigzag through these cones while carrying a net. When the rider approaches a bucket, she has to lower her net and try to scoop out a rubber ducky. You'll have one minute to run the course. The scores are based on how many ducks you get. Each one is worth five points."

It was our turn to go first.

"Just remember, Khadija, that timing is everything. You have to lower the net and scoop at the right time while Silver Moon gallops."

Khadija bit her lip. "Ready!"

She took off one way, but it seemed like Silver Moon had other plans and tried going a different direction. Silver Moon pranced around the course. There was no galloping! It was funny to watch, and even though Khadija didn't get any ducks, she got a round of applause.

Ryleigh did a lot better. She scooped up three ducks.

I went next and got six.

"Forty-five points," said Cassidy. "Good job."

Before the other team went, Aunt Jane announced the score again. "The score is tied 30–30. If the Core Four manages to scoop up ten ducks in three minutes, they'll win the Battle of the Bunks."

I groaned. "Avery's probably going to get ten ducks all on her own."

"Think positive," said Khadija. "It's not over until it's over."

"She's right," said Ryleigh. "We're still in it."

But I wasn't so sure.

"First up," said Aunt Jane, "is Esha."

Esha patted Queenie's back before she mounted her. She held the net close to Queenie's neck. By the time her turn was over, she had five ducks. Twenty-five points!

"It's over," I said as Jaelyn took her position. But Jaelyn had trouble controlling Blue. Blue kept running past the buckets before Jaelyn had time to lower her net. She only got one duck.

"I feel tension in the air," said Aunt Jane. "It all comes down to this last run. If Avery is able to snag four ducks, the Core Four will win this round and the Battle of the Bunks title."

I held my breath as Avery mounted Sapphire. Then I covered my eyes with my fingers. "I can't look," I said. "I'm too nervous."

Each time Avery scooped up a duck, the crowd counted out loud.

"One! Two!"

I took my hands away when I didn't hear them shout again.

About fifteen seconds passed before the crowd yelled, "Three!"

I ran over to Aunt Jane and looked at her stopwatch.

"Five seconds, four seconds, three seconds, two seconds . . ."

"Four!" the crowd yelled.

"Time," said Aunt Jane.

I felt like I had been punched in the stomach.

It was over. Avery had done it. The Core Four had won.

Aunt Jane put her arm around my shoulders. "You raced well, Ainsley. You should be proud of yourself and your team."

Even though we already knew the results, we waited for Layla to tally the points.

"The Core Four's combined total for this event was fifty lucky ducky points. The Four Horseketeers were able to scoop up nine ducks which gave them forty-five lucky ducky points.

That means ten points go to the Core Four!"

Then she updated the chalkboard.

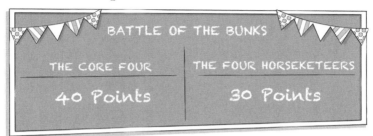

Everyone started clapping and cheering in the stands.

We walked over to the Core Four and shook their hands.

"Congratulations," I said. "You deserved it."

"Thanks," said Avery. "It was fun. Maybe we can have a rematch next year. A Battle of the Bunks Two?"

I nodded. "That sounds like fun."

Aunt Jane and Layla rushed over to us.

"We have a little surprise for you," said Aunt Jane. She held up a trophy that had Battle of the Bunks Champs written on the base. "I'm not sure how or why this whole battle started. We certainly have other contests here at Storm Cliff Stables. But for whatever reason, it seemed like it was needed. I'd just like to say how proud I am of both teams today for their honesty and integrity. Both teams displayed good sportsmanship."

Aunt Jane wiped away a tear.

She held the trophy above our heads. "I'd like to present this trophy to the Core . . ."

But Esha interrupted her. "Did you say honesty, Aunt Jane?"

Aunt Jane nodded.

Esha bit her lip. "Can we just have a few minutes, please? We need to discuss somethin'. It won't take long."

Esha even walked out of the huddle to find Carly and bring her into the group. Five minutes later, they came back over to us.

"We didn't win fair and square, Aunt Jane," said Avery.

Aunt Jane's smile disappeared. "Someone cheated? Say it isn't so."

"It ain't so, Aunt Jane," said Esha. "Let's just say there was a misunderstanding with Carly and a sack of salt."

Aunt Jane narrowed her eyes and motioned for Carly to step forward.

"Is this a story I need to know?" she asked.

Carly shrugged.

I stepped up. "Nah. Just typical camp stuff. It's all good."

Then Bree spoke up. "We can't accept the ten points for the cupcakes. It wouldn't be fair."

Layla erased ten points from their score. "Then it looks like a tie. Does everyone agree?"

No one said anything.

"All in favor of calling this Battle of the Bunks a tie, say, 'Aye.'"

The entire camp said "Aye" together.

Aunt Jane gave us a thumbs-up. "This is why

I love Storm Cliff Stables. You girls are always working together and working it out. I think I'm the luckiest camp owner in the world."

I rushed forward to hug her. "I think we're the luckiest campers in the world."

After we hugged, Aunt Jane bent over and scrunched her nose. "Um, think you want to tell me where those blue teeth came from?"

"Maybe next year," I said. "At Battle of the Bunks Two."